The Junior Novelization

Special thanks to Sarah Buzby, Cindy Ledermann, Vicki Jaeger, Dana Koplik, Ann McNeill, Emily Kelly, Sharon Woloszyk, Julia Phelps, Tanya Mann, Rob Hudnut, David Wiebe, Tiffany J. Shuttleworth, Gabrielle Miles, Rainmaker Entertainment, Walter P. Martishius, Carla Alford, Rita Lichtwardt, and Kathy Berry

Published in the United States by Random House Children's Books, a division of Random House, Inc., 1745 Broadway, New York, NY 10019, and in Canada by Random House of Canada Limited, Toronto. Random House and the colophon are registered trademarks of Random House, Inc.
ISBN: 978-0-307-93024-8
randomhouse.com/kids
Printed in the United States of America
10 9 8 7 6 5 4 3 2 1 First Edition

The Junior Novelization

Adapted by Molly McGuire
Based on the original screenplay by Elise Allen

Random House 🏠 New York

Chapter 1

"Go, Liah!"

Merliah Summers heard her friends cheering from the beach as she paddled her surfboard out into the ocean. In the distance, she spied the perfect wave.

Merliah turned her board toward the shore. As the wave swelled under her, she checked her balance and tried an aerial.

"Yes!" the young surfer cried as she nailed the trick.

Merliah waved at her best friends, Fallon and Hadley, and at her grandfather Break, all watching from the beach. There was nothing like a day on the waves: the warm sun on her back, the wind in her long pink-streaked blond hair, and the smell of the salty ocean water.

But the amazing setting didn't distract Merliah from the important competition she was surfing in—or from her rival, Kylie Morgan from Australia. Just as Merliah caught another wave, Kylie dropped in next to her, cutting her off.

Merliah focused and bent her knees. She zoomed in front of Kylie.

The girls zigzagged across each other's paths. Merliah answered Kylie's signature cutback with a flip of her own. She entered the tube of the wave with Kylie right behind her.

The crowd on the beach held its breath. Both surfers had talent, and this contest was just the latest in a neck-and-neck race that had been going on for the past year.

Merliah adjusted her feet to steer her board toward the shore. She pulled a final snap and rode the wave all the way to the shallows.

Break, Hadley, and Fallon splashed into the water to greet her. Break wore board shorts, and the girls were both in colorful two-piece swimsuits.

"I got one thing to say to you, Liah," Break told her.

Merliah grinned.

"Whoa?" she guessed.

Break grinned and nodded.

"Whoa!" He repeated the expression, which had been his favorite as long as Merliah could remember. A surfer himself, Break had raised Merliah and taught her everything she knew about the sport.

"You *thrashed* it, Merliah!" Fallon said. "You're taking this meet."

"Your run was great, too!" Merliah replied. Fallon was also a surfer, and had done well in an earlier heat.

"Wait!" Hadley said.

While Hadley was not as athletic as Merliah and Fallon, she was always ready to cheer her friends on. She closed her eyes and rubbed her temples.

"I'm seeing a vision . . . the two of you . . . holding surfboards . . . cuddling koalas . . . in Australia!" Hadley exclaimed.

The World Championship Surf Invitational was the biggest surfing contest of the year. It was scheduled to take place in Australia, and

Merliah had been training for it for months. Just thinking about competing gave her goose bumps.

Just then, Kylie sliced her board to a halt right in front of Merliah and her friends, sending up a huge spray of water.

"Hey!" Merliah cried.

"Ooooh, sorry," Kylie sneered. Her long reddish-brown hair hung down her back in damp waves. "Did I get you? My bad."

"I thought it was a nice carve," said Merliah. She turned to Fallon. "If she'd had more of those on the waves today, she might even have had a shot at beating me."

Kylie smirked.

"You mean the way I whupped you last week in La Jolla?" she challenged.

"Actually, I was thinking more about the way *I* beat *you* the week before, in Redondo," Merliah shot back.

Just then, the contest announcer's voice came through the speaker system.

"Listen up, dudes and dudettes. Our panel of judges has chosen our winners!"

Merliah linked arms with Fallon and took a deep breath. This was the moment of truth. If Merliah's name was called, she was headed to Australia for the World Championship Surf Invitational.

"Third place," the announcer's voice boomed. "Fallon Casey!"

"Yes!" Fallon shouted.

The announcer continued.

"Second place, Kylie Morgan!"

Merliah held her breath.

"And first place, Queen of the Waves, Merliah Summers!"

Merliah's face broke into a huge smile. She looked at Kylie, who wore an angry frown.

"These three surfers now advance to the World Championship Surf Invitational," said the announcer.

"Ahh! You won!" Hadley cheered. She threw herself at Merliah. "Group hug! Group hug! This is *huge*!"

Fallon and Break couldn't resist Hadley's excitement. They joined in and hugged Merliah.

Hadley stretched an arm toward Kylie, who

was still sulking over her second-place finish.

"You too, Kylie! Come on!" called Hadley.

But Kylie took a step back. She glared at Merliah.

"You were lucky, mate," Kylie said, "but your luck's gonna run out Down Under. That's *my* turf."

The Australian surfer turned on one foot and stormed up the beach.

Merliah untangled herself from her friends and watched Kylie walk away.

Fallon put an arm around Merliah's shoulders.

"She's just a little ray of sunshine, isn't she?" she said.

Merliah smiled halfheartedly.

All of a sudden, Merliah heard a familiar bark coming from the water. She turned around to see Snouts, her baby sea lion friend, swimming toward them.

"Snouts! Hey, what'd you think?" she asked.

Snouts clapped his front flippers eagerly and did a joyful leap into the air.

Break turned to Merliah. "I know someone who will be stoked for you," he said.

Merliah's face lit up.

"My mom! I'm going to tell her," she said excitedly. "See you later!"

Merliah grabbed her surfboard and ran back into the ocean, Snouts right behind her.

Chapter 2

When Merliah had paddled far enough into the ocean, she clutched the pink seashell necklace she always wore and closed her eyes.

"I wish to become a mermaid," she said.

Glittering magic swirled around her as her legs were replaced by a long, beautiful tail that sparkled with shiny pink scales.

The first time Merliah had made the transition to being a mermaid, she had been stunned. But now she was used to it.

Although Merliah had been raised as a human, her mom, Calissa, was a mermaid. Calissa was also the powerful magical queen of the underwater world of Oceana—which meant that Merliah was a mermaid princess with magical powers of her own.

Merliah had first learned about her mother and her own position as a mermaid princess a year earlier, when she had been summoned by the merfolk to help rescue Calissa. The queen's evil sister, Eris, had trapped her in an undersea whirlpool and tried to take over Oceana.

Luckily, Merliah had been able to defeat Eris and set Calissa free. Since then, Eris had been imprisoned in that very whirlpool, and Oceana had been safe.

Now, with the help of her seashell necklace, Merliah was able to live in both worlds.

Once her transformation into a mermaid was complete, Merliah grabbed the leash of her surfboard and dove gracefully to the bottom of the ocean.

She stashed her board in its usual spot behind some rocks and took off along the ocean floor.

"Race you to Oceana!" she said to Snouts, who followed happily.

As Merliah and Snouts swam toward the dazzling underwater city of Oceana, merfolk of all shapes and sizes bowed and waved to her. After all, she was their princess.

"Hello, Merliah!"

Merliah nodded and waved in return, grateful for such a warm greeting.

"Nice to see you!" she replied.

Suddenly, a group of pufferazzi fish swam directly in front of Merliah, snapping photos and pushing microphones into her face.

Being a mermaid princess had its perks, but sometimes the fame was a bit overwhelming.

"Princess Merliah!" one reporter shouted. "We're all wondering—how'd you do at the big surf meet today?"

"I'd be happy to tell you all about it," Merliah replied. "But first I want to tell my mom."

Merliah grabbed Snouts by a flipper and pulled him in front of her like a cuddly shield.

"Snouts can fill you in on the highlights, though! Thanks so much! Goodbye!" she called.

Merliah swirled her tail through the water and raced away from the crowd.

Chapter 3

Merliah arrived at the palace and swam right to her mother's bedroom, where Calissa and her pink dolphin friend, Zuma, were busy packing for a trip to the Mercropolis, the ancient center of the city of Aquellia.

It was almost time for the momentous Changing of the Tides ceremony, which only happened once every twenty years.

Calissa was a stunning mermaid with a long, shimmering tail, beautiful blond hair, and kind eyes. Merliah looked a lot like her.

Calissa held up a glittering hair comb and showed it to Zuma.

"I remember my mother gave me this before my first Changing of the Tides ceremony," she said wistfully.

Merliah entered the room.

"Mom?" she said as she swam toward her mother.

At the sound of her daughter's voice, Calissa whirled around.

"Merliah?"

Calissa swam to her daughter and wrapped her in a hug. Then she pulled back and examined Merliah at arm's length.

"Welcome back, Merliah," Calissa said. "How did it go? Did you win?"

"Well . . . ," Merliah began, drawing out the suspense. Then she grinned. "I won!"

"Wonderful!" Calissa cheered, and hugged her daughter again.

"Congratulations, Merliah," Zuma said.

"Thanks!" Merliah replied.

"I've been pulling out some special things to pack for the trip," said Calissa.

She put down the comb she had been holding and picked up a large, open-mouthed shell.

"What is it?" Merliah asked.

Calissa held the shell out to Merliah.

"It's a See Shell. You can see its owner's

memories." Calissa waved her hand over the mouth of the shell. "Show me the last Changing of the Tides ceremony," she commanded.

Merliah watched as a colorful mist floated out of the mouth of the shell and took shape. She gasped in amazement as a crystal clear image of a ceremony came into view.

She saw a large, elaborately decorated throne. A small group of merpeople were gathered together in front of it.

Suddenly, it all made sense.

"So *that's* Aquellia!"

"Yes," Calissa said. "The city where merfolk history began, deep in the waters off New Zealand."

Merliah listened closely.

"Every twenty years," Calissa continued, "a member of the royal family must return to Aquellia, sit atop the ancient throne, and regain the power to make Merillia."

Merliah gazed into the shell's holographic mist. She saw a beautiful young mermaid approaching the throne.

"That's you!" she cried to her mother.

Calissa nodded, remembering every detail of the momentous day.

"I was so nervous. Still, I took my place on the throne and spoke the ancient rite . . ."

Merliah looked from her mother to the mist. She watched as a younger Calissa recited the most important words in the merworld.

"With the changing of the tides,
Merillia power will arise.
The royal mermaid on the throne,
her fullest merself now is known.

". . . and then, at exactly midday," Calissa told her daughter, "it happened."

Merliah couldn't take her eyes off the hologram. She watched a ray of sun move across the floor of the Mercropolis, hitting the first ambassador's gem and sending a reflection to the next one. The reflection traveled brilliantly from gem to gem, until at last it hit the throne itself.

Calissa shut the See Shell with a click.

"When it was all over," she said, "I had the

power to make Merillia and give life to the sea."

Merliah looked at her mother in awe.

"That's amazing," Merliah whispered. "You must be so excited to do it again."

Calissa let out a sigh.

"I wish you could have the honor," she said. "The magic was so powerful, but it transformed my tail forever. I fear it would transform yours, too, and you would be unable to use your legs again."

"I can't even imagine," Merliah replied.

"And I would never ask you to do it." Calissa smiled and put an arm around her daughter. "I'm just thrilled you'll be there to watch."

Merliah felt a knot form in her stomach.

"Well...," she began. "Actually, the ceremony's the same day as the Invitational."

Calissa eyed her daughter. "And?" she asked warily.

Merliah hesitated.

"And so . . . I can't make it."

A look of disappointment came over Calissa's face.

"You'll just have to miss this one surf meet,"

said Calissa. "You are the princess of Oceana, Merliah. You must be at the ceremony."

But Merliah was not willing to give up her chance to win the World Championship Surf Invitational—or to beat Kylie.

"Kylie Morgan will be there!" she protested. "This will be my chance to prove I'm better than she is . . . *in front of the whole surfing world!*"

"True worth isn't measured in comparison to others," Calissa stated. "Life isn't a competition."

Merliah took a calming breath.

"Mom, please listen to me. I know you want me to see the ceremony, but I can't go!"

"Merliah," Calissa replied. "It's important to the merpeople of Oceana that their princess take an interest in the future of the ocean."

"But what about what's important to *me?*" Merliah asked. "Don't you even care?"

"Of course I do," said Calissa. "But you're being unreasonable!"

"Mom," Merliah pleaded. "Don't you see? I've been working for this my whole life. If you *really* care, you'll understand that—and be happy for me."

With a whip of her tail, Merliah turned and zoomed out of the room.

"Merliah! Come back!" Calissa called after her daughter. But it was no use.

Merliah was gone.

Chapter 4

On the day of the qualifying heats for the World Championship Surf Invitational, Merliah looked out at the beach from her spot on the waves. It was packed! Fallon and Hadley were there to cheer her on, and Kylie was already in the water.

As Merliah paddled out to catch another ride, she heard the announcer's voice over the loudspeaker.

"This final qualifying heat has been brutal, and it's not over yet!"

Kylie caught her next wave and executed a perfect trick.

The crowd on the beach cheered.

"Humdinger of a backside air reverse by Kylie Morgan!" the announcer cried. "Can anyone challenge those skills?"

Merliah nabbed her next wave and nailed an impressive 360 as she aimed for the shore.

"Merliah Summers answers with a three-sixty!" the announcer boomed. "It's a grudge match on the waves!"

The crowd went wild.

As Merliah paddled back in search of her next wave, Snouts popped out of the water and did a flip, happy to see his friend.

Merliah smiled at Snouts, then positioned her board perfectly, paddled, and caught a wave toward the shore. Kylie caught the same wave and rode high on its crest while Merliah cut into its trough.

Kylie grinned wickedly. "Say goodbye to first place, Merliah Summers!" she said. She sliced into the wave, getting too close to Merliah.

Merliah lost her balance and struggled to stay upright on her board. Then she had a brilliant idea. She bent over and pushed up into a handstand!

The crowd erupted into loud cheers. What a move!

"I can't believe this is real!" the announcer

said excitedly. "Merliah Summers shoots the tube on her *hands!*"

Merliah smiled to herself. But a handstand on a surfboard was no easy feat, and she soon toppled off her board into the water.

"Ohhh!" the announcer cried as Merliah went down. "Wild wipeout after a beauty ride! But Kylie Morgan's riding strong!"

An air horn blew, signaling the end of the heat.

"Surfers in!" the announcer called.

Back on the beach, Fallon and Hadley looked worried.

"Do you think she'll still move on after that wipeout?" Hadley asked.

Fallon bit her lip. "Not sure. Merliah has to get into the top three to move on, like I did in my heat. Think good thoughts."

Hadley nodded. Good thoughts were her specialty. She rattled off the first ones that came to mind.

"Kittens . . . ponies . . . sardines and jam."

Fallon raised an eyebrow.

"It's an acquired taste," Hadley remarked.

Chapter 5

Merliah tucked her board under her arm and trudged out of the water, frustrated with her performance.

"Merliah, wait up!" She turned at the sound of her name and was surprised to see Kylie splashing up behind her.

"You got something on your back," Kylie said with a slick smile. She reached out as if to brush something off Merliah's shoulder.

"Oh, wait—that's just my footprints, 'cause I stomped all over you!"

Merliah groaned.

"Very funny," she replied. "We'll see what happens tomorrow at the final."

"Mmm-hmm," Kylie agreed. "*If* you qualify."

The girls noticed a large group of reporters

and photographers running toward them.

"Excuse me," Kylie said smugly. "I'm guessing they want to talk to me about my killer technique." She raised her chin and walked proudly toward the group.

But the reporters hardly noticed Kylie. Instead, they brushed past her and surrounded Merliah.

"Merliah, look over here!" one shouted, holding a camera high above his head.

"That handstand move was amazing!" another reporter gushed. "Is that the first time you've done that on the board? And that wipeout—are you okay?"

Merliah was too stunned to answer. Kylie frowned and crossed her arms in disgust.

Then the announcer's voice came over the loudspeaker again and the crowd quieted.

"And the scores are in!" the announcer boomed. "Moving on from this heat to tomorrow's finals: Third place, Allie Mahoney! Second place, Merliah Summers. And first place...Kylie Morgan! Congratulations, surfers!"

The crowd gave loud applause. Kylie

prepared to accept her congratulations from the reporters. She put her hand over her heart and closed her eyes.

"Wow, I can't believe I won first place. Me. Kylie. The winner."

But when Kylie opened her eyes, her jaw dropped. The reporters and photographers were still gathered around Merliah! Kylie stomped her foot angrily.

Just then, a woman in a business suit broke through the crowd of reporters. Merliah recognized her as the famous businesswoman Georgie Majors. The woman pushed for a position next to Merliah.

"Merliah, what do you call that handstand move?" asked a reporter.

Merliah opened her mouth to answer, but Georgie spoke first.

"It's called the Summers Switcheroo, of course!" Georgie put an arm around Merliah's shoulders. "And we'll be featuring it in our new ad campaign for Wavecrest Surf Gear!" She turned to address Merliah. "That is . . . if you're interested in being our new spokesperson."

Merliah was speechless. "What? But you're Georgie Majors! You *created* Wavecrest! I wear your clothes all the time! I love them!"

Georgie chuckled. "And I love your spirit," she replied. "So what do you say? Will you do it? We can shoot our first layout at tonight's luau."

Merliah clapped her hands. "Are you kidding? Yes!"

Georgie slipped on a pair of designer sunglasses. "Dazzling. I'll see you then."

"I can't wait!" Merliah replied excitedly.

Georgie nodded and power walked off the beach, leaving the reporters to surround Merliah again.

Kylie saw her chance and bounded after Georgie.

"Ms. Majors! Ms. Majors!" she shouted, catching up with her. "I wanted to introduce myself." Kylie extended her hand. "I won that last heat. You know—me. Not Merliah."

But Georgie hardly seemed to notice Kylie. "I see. Congratulations," she said. It was obvious she wasn't interested.

Kylie wasn't one to give up. "I'm just saying,"

she continued, following Georgie like a puppy, "in case you wanted another spokesperson . . . or a different one . . . I can do handstands, too." She ran in front of Georgie and did a series of cartwheels and handstands. "See?" She plastered a big grin on her face.

"Impressive," Georgie said, and kept walking. "See you at the luau!" she called over her shoulder, leaving Kylie alone by the water.

"But I won the heat! I *won*!" Kylie called. She kicked the sand in frustration. "Ow! Sand in my eye!" She staggered and stubbed her toe on a rock. "Ow!"

She might have won the heat, but it was definitely not turning out to be Kylie's day.

Chapter 6

That afternoon, Calissa and Zuma swam into the majestic ancient ruins of the Mercropolis.

"The Mercropolis is stunning. It's an honor to be a part of this," Zuma said.

"I'm glad *you* see it that way," Calissa said, distracted. The fight with Merliah still weighed heavily on her mind.

"You can go talk to her, you know," Zuma suggested. "We're not far from the Australian coast."

Calissa paused, thinking it over. Maybe she *should* find Merliah and try to patch things up. But the queen's thoughts were interrupted by a voice calling her name.

"Calissa! Calissa!"

Calissa raised her head to see four gorgeous

mermaids swimming on the other side of the Mercropolis. The ambassadors had arrived! Their names were Mirabella, Renata, Selena, and Kattrin. Calissa smiled, her thoughts of Merliah temporarily forgotten.

The ambassadors were the merfolk who were closest to the royal family. They each represented an important area of the ocean, and each was as beautiful as she was unique.

Kattrin, the ambassador from Asia, zoomed up to Calissa first. Kattrin did everything quickly—including talking.

"Calissa, we're so glad you're here!" she said in a rush.

"Kattrin!" Calissa exclaimed.

"And this must be Zuma!" Kattrin said. She smiled at the pink dolphin.

"Nice to meet you," offered Zuma.

The other ambassadors finally caught up to speedy Kattrin, their aides trailing behind them.

"Isn't it glorious here at the Mercropolis?" asked Mirabella, the peace-loving ambassador of South America. "So open and beautiful and free. It has the perfect energy for the Changing of the Tides ceremony."

"It does, Mirabella," Calissa agreed. She loved Mirabella's knack for finding beauty in everything. "It's wonderful to see you."

"Calissa, you look stunning," remarked Selena, the Arctic ambassador.

"Never as stunning as you, Selena," Calissa returned, marveling at Selena's beauty. Selena was easily the most striking of the bunch, with the longest, most colorful tail and glorious blond hair. "Your tail is breathtaking."

Selena ran her fingers through her flowing hair. "I know. Look, the light dances off it when I swim." She twirled in the water, sending a shimmer of sparkles around her.

"Enchanting," Calissa replied. She turned to the fourth ambassador. "Renata, always a pleasure. This is Zuma," she said, gesturing to her dolphin friend.

Renata was the African ambassador. Dressed in red and carrying a spear, she was a warrior with a quiet strength about her. She nodded solemnly at Calissa.

Mirabella clasped Calissa's hands. "We need to catch up," she said excitedly. "There's a blissful spot at the top of the Mercropolis. We can see for miles."

"That sounds perfect," Calissa replied.

Kattrin raced ahead of them. "Meet you in two shakes of a mertail!" she called over her shoulder. She zipped through the water, leading the pack toward Mirabella's spot.

Zuma and Calissa followed.

"Weren't we going somewhere else, Your Majesty?" Zuma whispered.

"No, Zuma," Calissa replied. "Merliah knows where to find me if she really wants to. Come."

Zuma let out a sigh and followed the queen.

Chapter 7

That night, Merliah and her friends were on the beach for the evening luau. A large dock lined with small, brightly lit huts jutted out into the ocean.

Merliah was posing for her Wavecrest photo shoot. Fallon and Hadley skipped along the dock, admiring the dazzling reflection of the lights on the water as they made their way to the buffet line.

Hadley held out her plate and a server slapped a scoop of goop onto it. Hadley wrinkled her nose. "What's that?" she asked. "I think it's looking at me!"

"That's beetroot and poi, mate!" the server announced.

Hadley eyed her plate. "It's still moving. It

wants to escape." No way was she trying this stuff.

Fallon rolled her eyes. "They're delicacies of Australia and Hawaii," she said. "We should try some." She looked at the server. "A big helping for me, please."

On the other side of the luau, Merliah was too busy to eat. Cameras and lighting poles surrounded her.

"Like this?" Merliah asked, striking another pose. She wore a Wavecrest hoodie from the spring collection over her bathing suit.

Georgie hovered near the cameras, directing Merliah.

"I love your necklace!" Georgie called. "Unfortunately, it's a little distracting. I want everything you're wearing to be Wavecrest's latest and greatest. Try this on instead." She held out another necklace. "And you can swap out for this hoodie," she said, holding up a purple sweatshirt.

Merliah bit her lip. "Okay, but . . . ," she replied slowly. "I'd like to keep my necklace on, please. I never take it off."

Georgie nodded. "That's lovely. And thank you for asking so nicely."

Merliah breathed a sigh of relief. "You're welcome," she said.

Georgie wasn't finished. "But the answer is no," she said firmly. "You're a Wavecrest Surf Gear girl, you wear Wavecrest Surf Gear. You do want to be a Wavecrest Surf Gear girl . . . don't you?"

"I do!" Merliah answered quickly. She didn't want Georgie to think she was ungrateful. "It's a huge opportunity!" she added.

"Yes. It is," Georgie said.

Merliah thought for a moment. She didn't want to take off her necklace. But she didn't want to lose her opportunity with Wavecrest, either.

She carefully unclasped the necklace and dropped it into the pocket of her hoodie. She would put it back on after the shoot.

At the buffet, Hadley and Fallon made their way to a table, their plates piled high. Hadley dug in immediately.

"Ugh!" said Fallon. "How can you eat that?"

Hadley swallowed. "It's a local delicacy!" She pointed her fork at Fallon. "You were the one who told me to try it, remember?"

Fallon pushed her plate away. "That was before I tasted it! Blech!"

Hadley stuffed a big forkful into her mouth and closed her eyes. She loved it. She reached for Fallon's plate.

"Does that mean I can have yours?" she asked.

Fallon nodded.

Just then, Merliah approached. "Please tell me you have something to get this taste out of my mouth," said Fallon. "Breath mint, anchovies, a full head of garlic—anything."

"Can't help you with that one," said Merliah.

Fallon saw a server carrying a huge pitcher. She clutched her throat dramatically.

"Water!" she cried, and chased after him.

Merliah chuckled and turned to Hadley. "Do you mind holding my stuff while I finish the shoot? I'll just be a few minutes." Merliah held out the hoodie she had worn to the shoot, clutching the pocket carefully.

"Mmm . . . mmm-hmm!" Hadley exclaimed around a mouthful of food.

"Cool," Merliah said, handing Hadley the sweatshirt. "My watch and necklace are in the pocket, so please be careful that they don't fall out."

"Mmm-hmm," Hadley mumbled, diving in for her next bite.

Merliah hesitated for just a minute. Hadley didn't seem to be paying that much attention. But she decided not to worry.

"Thanks. Enjoy your . . . sludge."

Hadley nodded and rubbed her tummy. "Mmmm!"

Chapter 8

Kylie sat at the end of the dock, letting her feet dangle into the water. She didn't feel much like being at a party.

Suddenly, she spotted something shimmering on the water's surface.

A low voice came from the area of the shimmer. "My, aren't we the life of the party."

Kylie peered into the water.

"Observant, too, aren't you?" the voice chuckled.

Kylie couldn't see anything. "Where are you?" she asked the darkness.

"Look down," said the voice.

Kylie looked into the water below and spotted a shimmering rainbow fish.

"All I see is a fish," she said slowly.

The fish flashed a smile. "Bingo," he said.

Kylie leaped up from the dock and screamed. She put her hands out in front of her and backed away from the water.

"Brilliant," said the rainbow fish in an annoyed tone. "Get everyone's attention before I can tell you how to beat Merliah Summers in the tournament tomorrow."

Kylie took one step closer to the edge of the dock. "Wait—what did you say?"

The rainbow fish knew Kylie was hooked. "Well, the girl has a magical advantage," he replied. "I'm surprised you haven't figured that out for yourself."

Kylie looked confused.

"She has a necklace that gives her special powers," the fish continued. "You take the necklace, you take the powers."

Kylie put her hands on her hips. "A magic necklace?" she cried. "You're bonkers!"

The rainbow fish eyed her. "Am I? *You're* the one talking to a fish."

"Fair enough," agreed Kylie. "Okay, go on."

The rainbow fish swam closer. "If you want

to win," he whispered, "you'll get that necklace and bring it back here."

Kylie sat down. "How?" she asked. "I can't just pull it off her neck."

"It is a crime that I'm lower on the food chain than you. The necklace isn't *on* Merliah's neck; it's in the pocket of her hoodie, which is being held by her goop-devouring friend." He motioned toward Hadley.

Kylie thought for a moment. The fish made it sound so easy. But he was talking about *stealing*.

Irritated, the fish swam in a circle. "Forget it," he huffed. "I clearly mistook you for someone who actually wanted to win. Ta." He gave a small wave and dove under the water.

"Wait!" Kylie shouted.

The fish popped back up to the surface and raised an eyebrow. He did not have time for this.

Kylie drew a deep breath. "I'll get the necklace," she declared.

Chapter 9

Back on the beach at her photo shoot, Merliah struck pose after pose.

"Dazzling!" sang Georgie, clearly impressed. "Now one with the Summers Switcheroo!"

Merliah dove into a handstand, kicking her legs high in the air.

The crowd cheered at her signature move as camera flashes lit up the sky.

Meanwhile, Kylie snuck into one of the huts on the dock. She could hear the cheering from Merliah's nearby photo shoot.

She clenched her fists and saw Hadley standing in the buffet line, holding Merliah's hoodie under her arm.

"Please tell me I'm not too late for more beetroot and poi!" Hadley cried, holding up her empty plate for the astonished server.

"Are you kidding?" replied the server, eyeing the steaming trays in front of him. "I'm swimming in the stuff! You can have as much as you want."

Hadley grinned. "Yes! Load me up, please!"

Kylie watched as Hadley held out two plates. The server arched an eyebrow, then filled both plates and handed them to her.

But Hadley couldn't carry both plates plus Merliah's hoodie. She fumbled, trying to find a way to balance everything.

"Looks like I'll have to come back," she said to the server.

Kylie saw her chance. She swooped in next to Hadley.

"No worries!" she said cheerily. "Let me help you. I'll hold the hoodie while you take your"—she eyed Hadley's platefuls of gunk—"tasty-looking meal to your seat."

Hadley beamed. "Thanks, Kylie!" She handed over Merliah's hoodie and picked up her second plate. "That's the great thing about sports, you know?" Hadley chattered. "On the waves, you and Merliah are all in each other's face and I'll-get-you, but in real life, you're not about that at all."

Kylie nodded as she secretly reached into the pocket of the hoodie. She felt the beads of the necklace and wrapped her fingers around them.

Quick as an eel, she whisked the necklace from Merliah's pocket into her own, all the while smiling at Hadley.

"Nope. Not like that at all!" she said.

Once Hadley had sat down at a table with her two plates of food, Kylie handed her Merliah's sweatshirt.

"Enjoy your meal!" she said brightly, backing away. The whole operation had been as easy as taking kelp from a minnow.

"Thanks!" Hadley replied. "And good luck at the meet tomorrow. If you get nervous, they say you should imagine everyone in their underwear." She took a big bite and held up her fork. "Except at a surf meet, everyone's in their bathing suits, and that's a lot like underwear."

"Thanks for the tip," Kylie said, slowly inching away from Hadley. "But you know what? I'm feeling really good about tomorrow."

Kylie ran along the dock, searching the water for that telltale shimmer. Once she spotted it, she slowed down and reached into her pocket.

"Here it is," she said, pulling out Merliah's necklace and flashing it to the rainbow fish bobbing in the water. She took a deep breath. Suddenly, she felt uneasy. "Look," she said to the rainbow fish. "I just don't know about this. . . ." Her voice trailed off.

The fish waved a fin, as if to shoo Kylie's doubts away. "Fine, fine. Now put on the necklace and jump in the water."

Kylie pursed her lips uncertainly. "Jump in the water? But . . ."

The rainbow fish tapped an impatient fin on the water's surface.

"Do you know a better way to swim? If you want my help, you'll do what I say." He motioned toward the water. "In. Now."

Kylie closed her eyes. Before she could change her mind, she snapped the necklace around her neck and jumped off the dock.

Splash!

"Now repeat after me," the rainbow fish commanded when Kylie bobbed up to the surface for air. "I wish to become a mermaid."

Kylie looked confused but did as the rainbow fish requested.

"I wish to become a . . . *mermaid?*"

The moment the words came out of her mouth, a swirl of sparkling magic surrounded her. Everything glittered and glowed.

All at once, Kylie's legs transformed into a shimmering mermaid's tail.

"What's happening to me?" she cried.

"Now!" the rainbow fish ordered. "Follow me! All the way under!"

Kylie felt a wave of panic.

Maybe it hadn't been such a good idea to trust a talking fish after all.

"Wait!" she cried as she swam after him.

Chapter 10

Farther out in the ocean, Snouts watched Kylie's transformation in shock. He scanned the beach for Merliah, to warn her. But he was too far out to be able to reach her in time, so he flicked his tail and dove.

As the rainbow fish sped through the ocean, Kylie reached out a hand and grasped one of his fins. Her cheeks puffed out from holding her breath.

The fish turned to look at her. "You look like a greedy chipmunk," he said. "You can breathe underwater, you know."

Kylie's eyes widened. She let out her breath, sending a gust of air toward the rainbow fish.

"I *can* breathe underwater. How did this happen? How is this possible?" she asked.

"Same way it's possible for Merliah," the rainbow fish replied. "That's the first part of the secret to her success."

"There's more?" Kylie asked.

"You think *just* being a mermaid makes you a better surfer?" the fish scoffed. He pointed a fin at her enormous tail. "You really think you can lug that thing onto a board and hang one?"

Kylie blushed. "No, but . . ."

"You'll get all the answers you want," the fish replied. "But only if you stop asking questions and follow me."

The rainbow fish zoomed through the water. Kylie hesitated for just a moment before following him, flapping her new tail behind her.

On the beach, Merliah was searching frantically for her necklace.

"It *has* to be here!" she cried for the hundredth time since the photo shoot had ended. She paced the sand in the moonlight. Hadley and Fallon followed helplessly.

"We've looked everywhere," Fallon said.

Merliah brushed past her. "I just don't get it—how did it fall out of my pocket?"

Hadley wrung her hands. "I don't know. Merliah, I'm so sorry . . . ," she replied, close to tears. The necklace had been her responsibility, and now here they were, in the middle of the night, trying to find it.

Merliah turned to Hadley. "I'm not blaming you," she said softly. "I just need to find it!"

Fallon nodded. "You do," she agreed. "But we can't look any more tonight. The necklace could be right in front of us and we wouldn't see it. We'll see better in the morning."

But Merliah wouldn't give up. That necklace was everything to her.

"I *have* to find it! Let's keep looking."

She dropped to her knees and began sifting through the sand. She wouldn't rest until the necklace—her key to the mermaid world—was once again in her hands.

Chapter 11

Meanwhile, in the ocean, Kylie struggled to keep up with the rainbow fish. The ocean around her seemed to be turning darker and darker.

"This doesn't feel right," she said nervously.

The rainbow fish ignored her and pressed on. Not knowing the way back, Kylie had no choice but to follow.

Suddenly, she gasped. Up ahead she saw a giant, swirling orange whirlpool.

"Your Majesty," the rainbow fish announced, pausing at the mouth of the whirlpool. "I've brought you the girl. She'd like your help with her surfing."

Kylie inched closer. She heard a female voice from deep inside the whirlpool.

"Oh, I'd be happy to help. Come close, my

dear. Speak into the mouth of the whirlpool so I can hear you."

Kylie looked uncertain. There was something about the voice she just didn't trust.

"I want to be able to surf better than—" she began.

"I can't hear you, my dear. Lean closer," the voice commanded.

Kylie hesitated and then leaned over the rim of the whirlpool. "I want to be able to surf—" she said. But she just couldn't shake the feeling that something was very wrong. She turned to the rainbow fish. "You know what? I really just want to go—"

But before she could finish her thought, the rainbow fish darted toward her. He plowed into Kylie's stomach, sending her toppling backward— right into the whirlpool!

Kylie screamed.

As she fell, a mermaid with a fiery red tail whizzed past her out of the funnel. It was Merliah's evil aunt Eris!

"Freedom!" Eris cried. "Well done, Alistair," she said to the rainbow fish when she emerged from the whirlpool and took in her surroundings.

Alistair beamed.

"Still," the evil mermaid continued, her red hair matching the red of her tail, "you could have been speedier about it."

Alistair looked hurt. "But you said the Changing of the Tides ceremony isn't until noon tomorrow. I think I carried out your orders quite swiftly, all things considered," he huffed.

Eris eyed him. "Would *you* like to know how it feels to be trapped inside one of these whirlpools?" She twirled her finger, causing a tiny, threatening whirlpool to spin.

Alistair cowered. He knew better than to mess with the boss.

"Er . . . no . . . ," he stammered.

"Then don't try to tell me how swiftly you got me out," she growled.

"Yes, Eris. I mean, no. I mean, I won't." Alistair stumbled over his words.

"Good," Eris replied, making the tiny whirlpool disappear. She dusted off her hands and looked around. "Now come—we have to make sure *I'm* the one on the throne of Aquellia at noon. Then

I'll have the power to make Merillia, and the ocean will be mine!"

Eris threw back her head with a sinister laugh and swam off.

Alistair swam behind her, miffed. If it weren't for him, she would still be trapped in that whirlpool.

"'Then *I'll* have the power to make Merillia, and the ocean will be mine!'" he said in his best imitation of the evil mermaid. "Not that you could have done any of it without my help," he grumbled.

Just then, Eris wheeled around to face him. "*What* did you say?" she snarled.

Alistair cringed. Thinking fast, he darted toward a bed of kelp and grabbed some.

"Er, kelp?" he said, smiling charmingly. "I can't do anything without my kelp." He shoved a finful into his mouth and chewed. "Mmm, yum."

Eris gave him a threatening look. "Wise choice," she sneered. "Stick with that."

Nearby, Snouts quietly emerged from his hiding place in a seaweed bed and swam toward the whirlpool. He peered over the edge.

"Help!" cried Kylie. "Please! Someone help me!"

Snouts looked around to make sure no one could see him, and then he barked. *Arf!*

"Is someone there?" Kylie called. "Please, help me out of here!"

Snouts darted off in search of help.

Chapter 12

The next morning, Merliah, Fallon, and Hadley were still searching the beach for the necklace. They hadn't slept all night.

"It's *nowhere*!" cried Merliah.

Suddenly, a strange look came over her face. She walked out to the edge of the dock.

"Liah?" said Fallon. "Don't freak out on us."

"I'm not," replied Merliah. "It's the ocean . . . it feels . . . wrong somehow."

Just then, Snouts popped out of the water, barking to get Merliah's attention.

"Snouts!" cried Merliah. "Something's going on down there, isn't it?"

Arf! Arf! Snouts nodded and patted the surface of the water with one of his flippers.

Merliah nodded, understanding. "Here, too.

My necklace is gone," she said. "It disappeared last night."

Arf! Arf! Arf! Snouts barked frantically.

Merliah frowned. "It's all connected, isn't it? What happened?"

Snouts treaded water for a minute. He looked around and grabbed some seaweed with his mouth. He flipped it onto his head, making a wig of long hair. He rose out of the water on his tail and shimmied his body across the surface, tossing his seaweed hair back and forth and strutting.

Merliah studied him. Suddenly, she had it! Snouts looked an awful lot like someone they knew. She glanced at Fallon and Hadley, who had joined her at the water's edge.

"Girl," Fallon said, laughing. "If I didn't know better, I'd swear that sea lion was pretending to be—"

"Kylie," Merliah said, her face serious. "Snouts, are you saying Kylie has something to do with my necklace?"

Snouts clapped his flippers together.

Fallon stopped laughing.

"That's so funny!" Hadley chimed in. "I was with Kylie last night when I was holding your hoodie!"

Merliah looked at Hadley. "You were with Kylie?"

"Why didn't you tell us that last night?" Fallon asked.

Hadley shrugged. "It didn't seem important. She only held the hoodie for a second so I could balance my plates."

Merliah spun around. "She *held* the *hoodie*?" she cried.

Hadley looked at Merliah with a confused expression. "You keep repeating what I said. Did you get water in your ears yesterday?"

Merliah shook her head, trying to clear her thoughts. This couldn't be happening.

"I have to go down there," she declared.

"How?" Fallon asked, concerned. "If she has the necklace, you can't become a mermaid."

Hadley clucked her tongue. "She *is* a mermaid, silly, just like before she got the necklace."

Merliah nodded. "Right. I can still breathe underwater," she said. "I just won't have a tail."

Snouts spun in the water, shaking off his seaweed wig.

Wasting no time, Merliah dove below the waves. Cautiously, she took a deep underwater breath, just to make sure she still could. Satisfied, she surfaced again and called to Hadley and Fallon.

"Wish me luck. If everything goes well, I'll be back for the final heat this afternoon."

Merliah wrapped her arms around Snouts, and the pair headed into the ocean.

Chapter 13

Later that morning, Eris and Alistair were swimming toward Aquellia.

Alistair huffed and puffed, trying to keep up. "I wonder if I could trouble Your Majesty to slow down just a tad. . . . I'm flapping my fins so fast, I'm starting to chafe," he whined.

Eris whipped around and towered over him. "Are you complaining?" she asked.

Alistair shrank under her gaze.

"N-n-no. . . . Complaining? Me?" he stammered nervously.

Eris narrowed her eyes one more time and then kept going.

Alistair followed, trying to calm his nerves. Suddenly, he gasped.

In the shadows that surrounded them, several

pairs of glow-in-the-dark eyes stared out at him and Eris.

"Madame . . . Madame . . . ," he whispered.

Eris kept moving. If she sensed danger, she didn't show it.

Alistair swallowed nervously as a circle of large fish rose from the ocean floor. They had huge teeth, and their eyes were positioned on top of their flat heads. Poisonous barbs stuck out of their tails, giving off electric shocks.

Alistair gulped. Stargazers.

He tried not to panic as the stargazers surrounded him. Their eyes glowed. Their teeth gleamed in the dark ocean water. Electricity sizzled along their barbs, sending Alistair into a tizzy.

"Eris!" he shouted. "Eris!"

Eris whirled around.

"Honestly, Alistair, what is it this ti—" She stopped short and eyed the stargazers. "Well, what have we here?"

Electricity jolted from one stargazer's broad, flat back to another.

"Hmm," murmured Eris. "That *is* impressive.

And . . . are those barbs poisonous as well?" she asked one of the fish.

The fish gave a nod.

"Wonderful," Eris remarked. "Tell me, which one of you is in charge?"

A stargazer swam out from the circle.

"I am," he said, in an impressively deep voice. "And I don't like intruders. You and your pet will turn back immediately."

Alistair balked. "Her *pet*?" he squawked, clearly insulted. "Well, I never!"

One of the stargazers gave him a menacing stare.

Alistair went white with fear.

"Arf! Arf!" he said, playfully rolling over like a harmless puppy. "Look, I'm rolling over!"

Eris addressed the lead stargazer once again. "I'm afraid this is the fastest way to where I need to go," she said. "I will, however, make *you* an offer: you allow me and my pet to pass, and I'll allow you to become my loyal servants and carry out my bidding."

The stargazer laughed low in his throat. Electricity sizzled along his barbs.

"And *why* would we do that?"

Eris grinned meanly. "Oh, I was hoping you'd ask that. I had a year in a whirlpool with nothing to do but practice my skills, and I've been dying to try them out."

"Er . . . madame," Alistair began. "I'm not sure it's a good idea to make these guys angry."

A nearby stargazer growled.

"Last chance, mermaid," said the lead stargazer to Eris. "Get out."

Eris raised an eyebrow, challenging the stargazer to battle.

The fish gave off an electric flash and lunged for Eris, but she blasted him with a burst of magic. "From your deepest, darkest fear, your nightmare terror now appears!" she chanted.

A colorful cloud of smoke surrounded them. *Poof!*

When the smoke cleared, a tiny green fish swam around Eris's tail. The fish looked terrified.

The little fish opened his mouth to speak and a familiar low, booming voice came out. "Hey! What's going on! What happened to me?"

Eris had turned the lead stargazer into a

teensy green fish! The evil mermaid smiled, satisfied with her work.

"You, my friend," she said icily, "have just had the honor of being the first to experience my newest magic blast, which makes your worst nightmare come true."

The stargazer panicked. "No! Turn me back to normal! You've got to!" he cried.

Eris chuckled. "Oh, I don't 'got to' do anything," she said.

Then she turned to face the other stargazers. "But I do have plenty of nightmares to go around, and I am *very* eager to see them in action. What do you think? Would you care to join your leader, or would you rather follow me?"

The stargazers looked at their leader, now the size of a small shell, and swam toward Eris. They bowed to her to show their loyalty.

"Wise choice," Eris said. "Come then— Aquellia awaits."

She swam regally through the water, the stargazers in line behind her.

Chapter 14

Meanwhile, Merliah and Snouts raced through the deepest part of the ocean. Finally, they reached the whirlpool where Kylie was trapped.

"Help! Help me, please!" Kylie called from inside.

Merliah swam to the edge of the whirlpool. "Oh, no," she murmured. "Kylie?"

"Merliah?" Kylie shouted back. "Merliah, is that you?"

"Yes, it's me! Don't worry, I'm going to get you out of there," Merliah promised.

"How?" Kylie called. "It's swirling so fast, I can't even move."

"What happened? How did you get in there?" Merliah asked.

"This voice told me to lean inside. . . . I tried

Merliah and Kylie are the best surfers in Malibu!

Merliah's mother, Calissa, uses a See Shell to show
Merliah the Changing of the Tides ceremony.

Kylie is jealous when Merliah gets all the attention.

Kylie turns into a mermaid!

Oh, no! The evil Eris traps Kylie in a whirlpool.

Merliah and Kylie escape the whirlpool together.

The ambassadors prepare for the
Changing of the Tides ceremony.

Eris turns Calissa's tail to stone!

Merliah and her friends will stop at nothing to defeat Eris.

Merliah and Kylie push Eris off the throne.

Kylie saves the Changing of the Tides ceremony!

The ceremony transforms Merliah into
an amazing mermaid!

Merliah rescues Kylie.

The wicked spell is broken—and Eris is defeated!

Merliah makes Merillia while Kylie catches a wave.

Merliah and Kylie celebrate together!

to get away, but the talking fish . . ." Kylie tried to explain what had happened, but even to her it sounded ridiculous. "Merliah, am I dreaming? This is all crazy!"

"You're not dreaming," she assured Kylie. "And it's not crazy. What happened with the talking fish?"

"He pushed me. And when I fell inside, this *mermaid* burst out! But she was an evil-looking mermaid. Is that possible? I thought mermaids were supposed to be nice . . . and fictional. . . ."

Merliah sighed. Eris was on the loose.

"The whirlpool needs someone else to be inside, and then it can release its prisoner," Merliah said, thinking out loud.

It made perfect sense: When Merliah had escaped the whirlpool's grasp, it was because Eris fell in. And now Eris had escaped because Kylie was inside.

Merliah turned to Snouts. "Maybe I could make the whirlpool *think* it has another prisoner, and that means the only way to get Kylie out"— she swam to the edge of the whirlpool—"is for me to go in!" she called down to Kylie.

65

"What?" Kylie cried. "You can't! I won't know how to get *you* out."

But Merliah was already putting her plan into action. She inspected nearby seaweed plants, pulling on them to test their strength. She selected the toughest ones and began to tie them together.

"You won't have to," she called to Kylie. Her hands worked furiously. "*I'll* get me out!"

"How?"

"A leash!" Merliah shouted, holding up the long rope she had fashioned out of seaweed. "Like what we use on our surfboards!"

Merliah swam over to a large rock. She tied one end of the seaweed leash tightly around the rock. Then she tied the other end around her ankle and took a deep breath.

"Okay, Snouts . . . keep an eye on the leash. If it breaks, I'm in trouble."

Snouts wrinkled his brow, looking concerned.

Merliah scratched him behind his ears. "I know, but there's no other way. I can't let her stay in there."

Snouts nuzzled Merliah and bravely puffed

out his furry little chest.

Merliah swam to the lip of the whirlpool and plunged in headfirst. As soon as she dove in, Kylie popped out—just as Merliah had predicted.

"Yes!" cried Kylie, relieved to be free. But then she remembered that Merliah was still trapped.

"Merliah!" she called into the depths.

Inside the whirlpool, Merliah looked around. She heard Kylie call her name from above.

"I'm here!" Merliah replied. She held on to her leash with both hands and tried to pull herself out of the hole. She struggled and tugged, but the swirling water was too powerful.

"The current's even stronger than I remember," Merliah shouted toward the surface. "I can't climb out!"

Snouts and Kylie exchanged a worried look. Then they heard a noise.

Snap!

Snouts looked at the end of Merliah's leash that was tied around the rock. It was starting to give way! He yelped.

Kylie turned to see the weakening leash. "Oh,

no!" she cried. Merliah was in danger!

Snap!

The last bit of leash gave way and shot toward the whirlpool.

Kylie lunged, grabbing the leash just before the whirlpool swallowed it—and Merliah—for good.

Merliah felt the leash loosen and then suddenly tighten again. "What's happening?" she called.

"It's okay! I've got you," called Kylie. She held tight to the leash and braced her foot against a rock. "Try to climb! I'll pull."

She heaved the seaweed rope, but she couldn't move Merliah.

Snouts clamped onto the leash with his teeth and pulled, too.

Kylie smiled. "*We'll* pull!" she said. Then she heard Merliah's voice from below.

"I can't!" cried Merliah.

"What?" Kylie called to Merliah. "Since when does the Queen of the Waves give up?

Merliah smiled. Kylie had a point. She steeled herself and attacked her climb again.

With Snouts and Kylie's help, Merliah made steady progress, until she finally burst out of the whirlpool and landed on the ocean floor.

Kylie and Snouts dropped the leash and raced toward Merliah. They collapsed in a happy—and exhausted—hug.

But there was no time for celebration.

Behind them, the whirlpool gave a huge, hungry growl. It sparked and spun faster, swirling and churning into a giant vortex!

"Swim away!" Merliah yelled.

The three swam as fast as they could and dove behind a large rock for cover. They peered out just in time to see the whirlpool implode, letting off sparks like an enormous fireworks display. The sea floor shook as another implosion sucked everything toward an empty black hole.

Then, suddenly, the suction force died down, and the sea became quiet once again.

Chapter 15

Merliah took a deep breath and looked at Kylie. For the first time, she noticed that Kylie had a mermaid tail.

"Wow!" Merliah exclaimed.

Kylie blushed.

"Yeah. I'm kind of feeling the same thing," she said.

Merliah tried to put the pieces of the story together.

"Did you know? Is that why you took the necklace?"

Kylie shook her head.

"No, I had no idea. It was the fish. The talking fish. How could there be a talking fish?" She threw up her hands. "What am I saying? I look like a talking fish."

Kylie shook her head again, waving everything away.

"Forget it. It doesn't matter. I never should have taken your necklace," she said. "I just want to go home and forget this ever happened."

She reached behind her neck and unclasped the necklace.

"Here," she said, handing it back to Merliah.

"Thank you," Merliah replied.

Merliah felt so relieved to have the necklace back that it almost didn't matter what had happened. She ran her fingers over the seashell.

Arf! Arf!

Snouts worriedly circled Merliah's tail.

Merliah looked up. Kylie's tail had disappeared and she was struggling to hold her breath.

Without the necklace, Kylie was a regular human. She couldn't breathe underwater!

Merliah lunged toward Kylie and quickly refastened the necklace around her neck.

"You have to say 'I wish to become a mermaid!'" she cried.

Kylie said the words with her last breath. She was again surrounded by a cloud of shimmering magic. As she swirled around, her tail returned and she was able to breathe underwater again.

"Are you okay?" asked Merliah. "I wasn't even thinking.

"Me neither," said Kylie. "Maybe I'll just hold on to the necklace until we get back."

"Good idea," replied Merliah. "Snouts will take you. I have to stay down here."

"Why?" Kylie asked.

"The mermaid from the whirlpool is Eris, my aunt," Merliah explained.

Kylie raised an eyebrow.

"Your *aunt*?"

Merliah nodded.

"We're not close. If she's free, she'll try to stop my mom from recharging her power to make Merillia in the Changing of the Tides ceremony."

"I have no idea what you just said," Kylie replied, looking confused.

"Merillia is the life force of the sea," Merliah explained. "Unless I do something before midday, my aunt will find a way to control the entire ocean and enslave every living thing in it."

Kylie thought for a minute.

"Then I'm going with you," she declared.

Merliah shook her head.

"Kylie, we're thousands of feet underwater. This isn't exactly your element."

But Kylie wouldn't give up.

"My element? I'm a surfer. The ocean is my life. If your aunt is going to hurt it, I want to help stop her." She met Merliah's gaze. "Besides, I think you saved my life twice in the last five minutes. I owe you."

"I can't let you do it. It's too dangerous," Merliah insisted.

Kylie brushed her off.

"Didn't you say we only had until noon? We're wasting time talking."

Snouts did a happy dance in the water.

Kylie smiled.

"I think the sea lion agrees with me," she said.

"That's Snouts." Merliah paused. "Okay. You're right. We have to hurry. Let's go."

The three took off through the water.

But without her tail to speed herself along, Merliah fell farther and farther behind.

"Um, Kylie?" she called.

Kylie looked over her shoulder and doubled back.

"Oh—sorry," she said, reaching toward Merliah and grabbing her hand. "I'll drive, you navigate."

Merliah grinned. "Perfect."

Together, they set out for Aquellia.

Chapter 16

At the Mercropolis, Calissa, Zuma, and the ambassadors were busily preparing for the Changing of the Tides ceremony. It was set to begin in less than an hour, and they were putting the sacred gems in position.

Kattrin went first. She held up an emerald the size of a softball. "For the love and life of the ocean, I present the Emerald of the East!" She zipped forward and put the emerald in its proper spot.

Calissa nodded and waved a hand toward Selena. Selena raised a diamond the same size as Kattrin's emerald. It glistened in the sunlight. "For the love and life of the ocean, I present the immeasurably beautiful Kaleidoscopic Diamond of the North."

She admired her own reflection in the stone's clear surface for just a moment. Then she lowered it into place. Next, Mirabella showcased an enormous aquamarine gem.

"For the love and life of the ocean, I present the Aquamarine of the South, with color as deep, clear, and vast as the ocean itself."

She raised her stone for all to see and then anchored it into position.

Last, Calissa turned to face Renata.

The silent warrior displayed a huge purple amethyst. Renata nodded solemnly at the others and rested the stone in its spot.

"For the love and life of the ocean," she said, "I present the Amethyst of the East."

With all the major gems in place, the ambassadors joined hands and began to chant.

"Across the globe,
From sea to sea,
We bring these gems
All here to Thee."

"Thank you, ambassadors. As we await the

midday sun, let us enjoy together a ceremonial tea," Calissa suggested.

Just then, they heard a voice.

"You're not setting a place for me?" Eris emerged from the shadows.

The ambassadors gasped.

"Eris," Calissa replied coolly.

"And I brought guests," Eris announced.

On cue, the stargazers—and Alistair—slipped from the shadows. They surrounded the mermaids.

Calissa didn't waver. "I don't know how you escaped, Eris, but you will *not* interfere with the Changing of the Tides ceremony."

Eris clasped her hands and pretended to think. "I wonder . . . if I did, would it be your worst nightmare?"

Sensing the nature of Eris's threat, the ambassadors and their aides gathered behind Calissa, ready to protect their queen.

"You have one chance to end this peacefully, sister," Calissa continued. "Turn back and leave us. Now."

"Hmm, let me think about that one." Eris

cocked her head, weighing her sister's words. "No," she replied firmly. She motioned to the stargazers. "Go."

At Eris's command, the stargazers rushed forward. The ambassadors and their aides prepared for battle.

Alistair scampered behind a rock.

Calissa fired a blast of magic, which Eris easily ducked.

"I was always faster than you, sister," Eris cackled. She shot a blast in Calissa's direction.

Calissa dodged it. "Unfortunately, not smarter—*sister*."

The two continued to battle each other while the ambassadors and their aides fought off the stargazers.

"You don't enjoy a fight like I do—that's your problem," Eris said to Calissa.

"I don't *try* to fight, but I will defend the ocean," Calissa replied with steel in her voice. She heard a familiar battle cry. She turned just in time to see Renata lunge at a stargazer with a metal lance. The lance made contact with the fish, which shocked Renata with an electric charge. Calissa looked over at Renata.

Now that Calissa's attention was on Renata, Eris seized her chance. "Compassion is your downfall, sister," she said icily, hurling a bolt of magic in Calissa's direction.

Calissa whirled around, but she was too late—Eris's latest blast wrapped itself around the queen, causing her tail to grow heavy.

"My tail!" Calissa cried. Feeling as heavy as an anchor, she screamed in horror and sank toward the ocean floor.

"Your nightmare has come true!" Eris thundered.

Chapter 17

Zuma swam to Calissa's aid, ducking behind pillars and statues to stay hidden from Eris and the stargazers.

Meanwhile, the ambassadors rallied for a counterattack.

"Get her!" Kattrin called. She darted past the stargazer guarding the evil mermaid.

"Oh, your turn?" Eris asked. She zapped Kattrin with a magic blast and slipped past her, headed straight for the other ambassadors.

One by one, she blasted them all.

"Welcome to your worst nightmares, ambassadors. Let's see . . . what frightens you the most?"

A giant cloud of magic engulfed the ambassadors. When it cleared, Kattrin was the first to speak. "Whaaaat haaaave youuuuu dooooone?" she moaned slowly. The usually speedy ambassador now moved and spoke as if she were made of lead.

"Taken your speed, apparently," Eris said matter-of-factly. She loved a good nightmare. She motioned to one of the stargazers.

The fish swam toward Kattrin and plucked her up like a cat carrying a kitten.

Eris turned to Renata, the brave warrior, as the magic cloud around her lifted. She too looked the same—almost. But instead of standing proud and tall, she seemed to be afraid of everything around her.

Eris swam up to Renata. "Boo!" she shouted in her face. Renata screamed and ducked her head. At Eris's command, another stargazer captured her.

The beautiful Selena's cloud disappeared next. She instinctively raised her hand to her face and opened her mouth in horror.

"Need a visual?" Eris asked. She snapped her fingers and a stargazer shoved Selena in front of a reflective gem. Selena took one look at her reflection and screamed. Her face had been transformed into that of a hideous monster.

Eris swam over to Mirabella, the last of the ambassadors to emerge from her magic cloud. "Well, look at this!" Eris declared.

Mirabella looked around, horrified. She was trapped in a force field. She tried to push on it. But it was no use.

"Get me out of here!" she cried. "I can't stand being closed in!"

"Oh," started Eris, "I think I'd much rather *enhance* the experience."

She motioned to the stargazers. They lifted a heavy metal cage from the ocean floor and shoved the other ambassadors and their aides inside. Then, using their prongs, they gave the cage an electric charge, causing it to buzz and crackle dangerously.

Now that the fighting was over, Alistair came out from his hiding place.

"And just like that, Eris has defeated you all," he taunted the ambassadors. "You might say it's . . . *shocking*." He chuckled at his own joke.

Eris glared at him. "Don't you think that's

something *I* would have wanted to say?" she hissed.

"Oh. Sorry," Alistair said. He waved his fin graciously. "But you could tell them the part about how with Calissa at the bottom of the ocean, you're the only member of the royal family here to sit on the throne at midday and get the power to make Merillia." He stopped short. "Or . . . did I just give away that part, too?"

In their cage, the ambassadors gasped. Alistair was right. With her heavy tail, Calissa would never make it to the throne in time, and Merliah was nowhere to be found. Eris would take control of the ocean after all.

Chapter 18

On the ocean floor, Calissa struggled to move her heavy tail. But no matter how hard she tried, it wouldn't budge. She was trapped.

Just as she stopped moving, she heard a familiar voice.

"Calissa!"

"Zuma!" Calissa exclaimed, delighted to see the pink dolphin. "Oh, thank goodness."

She grabbed hold of Zuma's tail. "Swim with all your might," she commanded.

Zuma tried, but she couldn't budge the queen. "I'm so sorry. I can't," Zuma said.

"My tail is so heavy I can't move," Calissa replied. "Which means I can't get to the throne, and Eris will." She hung her head in despair.

Zuma frowned. "She'll have the power to

make Merillia," she said. "She'll rule the ocean for twenty years."

"Go," Calissa ordered. "Get more help. Enough that you can drag me to the throne. We can't let Eris take over."

Zuma had a thought. "Perhaps if I could find Merliah . . ."

Calissa's eyes lit up. "Yes! Find her! Find her and bring her here—quickly!"

"Yes, Your Majesty." Zuma darted off in search of Princess Merliah.

Meanwhile, Merliah, Kylie, and Snouts swam quickly toward Aquellia, looking for any sign of Eris.

Suddenly, Merliah stopped short. "My mom . . . she's in trouble," she said. "I can feel it." She pulled Kylie's hand, urging her to get moving. "Hurry! That way—and deep!"

The girls dove toward the ocean floor, swimming even faster.

Slam!

They ran smack into Zuma.

"Merliah!" Zuma exclaimed. She looked closely at Merliah. "Your legs!"

Merliah shrugged. "It's a long story," she said.

Then Zuma noticed Kylie for the first time. She looked at Kylie's tail and then at the necklace around her throat.

"Aren't you—?"

"Pleased to meet you," said Kylie, "talking pink-sparkly-dolphin-creature."

Zuma gave Kylie a quick nod, then turned to Merliah.

"Your mother . . . she's in terrible danger. Eris has sunk her to the bottom of the ocean, and she's stuck there!"

"I knew it!" Merliah cried. "We can help. Can you take us to her?" she asked Zuma.

"Yes. Hurry!" Zuma replied.

In Aquellia, the ambassadors knew they needed help. If Eris took the throne at midday, all of Oceana would be under her control.

Renata looked from Eris to the other ambassadors and back. She gave a small, frightened cry.

Mirabella understood. "We have to stop Eris."

"Hooooowwwww?" Kattrin asked. It was killing her to be in slow motion. She reached an arm out to the bars of the cage. A bolt of electric current started to buzz toward her, causing her to slowly pull her hand back.

Selena shook her head. "I don't think we should stop Eris, even if we could."

"Whyyyy?" drawled Kattrin.

"Calissa's at the bottom of the ocean," Selena explained. "If no member of the royal family sits on the throne at noon and gains the power to make Merillia, the ocean will die."

Chapter 19

Calissa struggled against the weight of her tail. There had to be a way to lift herself off the ocean floor. She wrapped her arms around a nearby rock and heaved, willing her body to rise through the water.

But it was no use.

Just then, Calissa saw shadows moving across the water—and they were headed in her direction. Unsure who it might be, she prepared herself for a fight.

"Mom?"

Calissa's heart surged with hope when she recognized the voice.

"Merliah?" she called.

Merliah rounded a corner with Zuma, Kylie, and Snouts trailing behind her. She rushed to her mother. "Are you okay?" she asked.

"I will be," Calissa replied. "Once we get me off the ocean floor."

Merliah hung her head. "I'm sorry. I never should have gone to the Invitational."

Calissa cupped her daughter's chin in her hand. "I'm sorry, too. After all, you're not only a merprincess. I should have realized how important your human life is to you, too— including your love of surfing. Please don't blame yourself."

Kylie rushed forward. "This is all *my* fault." She looked at Calissa. "I'm Kylie, the one who stole Merliah's necklace. Blame me."

Calissa's mouth dropped open. Merliah's necklace—stolen? She shook her head. "None of that matters right now," she said. "There are four of you—if you all work together, you can pull me up and place me on the throne in time for the ceremony."

"But what about Eris and the stargazers?" Zuma asked.

"We'll find a way past them," Calissa replied. "The most important thing is getting me on that throne. Are you ready?"

The four friends each took hold of Calissa. It would take every ounce of strength they had.

"Okay," Calissa said, taking a deep breath. "Here we go. One . . . two . . . three . . . swim!"

They pulled with all their might. But it wasn't enough.

"It's not working," Kylie said sadly.

"It *has* to work!" cried Calissa. "Try again! One . . . two . . . three . . ."

The four heaved against the weight of Calissa's tail. Still nothing.

Merliah hated to admit defeat, but some things were just impossible.

"Mom—" she said gently.

"No," Calissa interrupted her. "We can't give up. We can't let Eris sit on that throne and gain the power of Merillia! We can't let her take over the ocean!"

"No . . . we can't." Merliah sighed. Her mother was right. But that didn't change the fact that they couldn't move her.

"So try again! Everyone get ready!" Calissa commanded.

"Mom, this isn't going to work," said Merliah.

"Yes, it will!" Calissa insisted. "It has to!"

But Merliah had another idea.

"No, Mom. The only way to stop Eris from taking over is if another member of the royal family performs the ceremony."

Calissa knew that her daughter wanted to perform the ceremony herself.

"Merliah . . . ," she began.

Merliah put up a hand in protest. Her mind was made up.

"I have to do it. It has to be me," she said firmly.

"If you do it, your legs will become a tail forever," said Calissa. "You will never walk or surf again."

Merliah pursed her lips. "I know. But I'm the princess of Oceana. It's my duty. And it's my choice." She turned to her friends. "I'll need your help."

Kylie swam forward. "You're really going to do this, Liah?" she asked.

"You're risking everything to do what's right. You really think I'm going to let you one-up me?" said Merliah with a twinkle in her eye.

Kylie grinned. "Good one. I've got your back, Princess."

"I do, too," seconded Zuma.

Snouts gave a low bow.

"So what's the plan?" Kylie said, getting down to business.

Merliah shrugged. "Trust my instincts. Beyond that . . . I have no idea."

Chapter 20

Merliah, Kylie, Zuma, and Snouts stole into the Mercropolis unseen. They hid behind a large bed of kelp.

Merliah took in the scene—the trapped ambassadors, the electrified cage, the awful stargazers, and Eris watching over it all.

"In just a moment," Eris said to Alistair, "I'm going to sit on that throne. At exactly midday . . ."

By now, Alistair knew the rest by heart. "A shaft of sun will shine down and make its way to the Emerald of the East. From there, it will reflect off all the gems until it hits the throne and gives you the ultimate power you deserve."

For once, Eris looked pleased. "Precisely," she purred. "And *your* job is to make sure nothing gets in the way."

Alistair rubbed his fins together. He could practically taste their victory. "What could possibly get in the way?"

"So your job should be simple," Eris replied. "But if anything *does* go wrong, I will hold you personally responsible. Understand?"

She spun a tiny whirlpool of dark magic with her index finger as a reminder of the damage she could cause.

Alistair took the hint. "I understand."

"Good," said Eris. Satisfied, she swam off to the ceremony.

Merliah let out a breath she didn't even know she'd been holding. From their hiding spot in the kelp bed, she and her friends had heard everything.

"So let me get this straight," said Kylie. "It's the four of us against a gang of electric fish with super-sharp teeth, plus your aunt, who can point to us and make our worst nightmares come true."

Merliah nodded. "Pretty much, yeah."

Kylie shook her head. "That's not even a fair fight." She grabbed a handful of kelp. "We should use this kelp to tie our arms behind our backs, to give them a sporting chance," she said sarcastically.

Merliah's face lit up. "Kylie, you're a genius!" she exclaimed.

Kylie laughed. "What? Merliah, that was a joke."

"The most brilliant joke ever! It gave me an idea," said Merliah. "Are you ready? Two words: surf's up."

A few minutes later, Merliah and her friends were ready to put their plan into action. "Remember," said Merliah, "the stargazers' eyes are on top of their heads. Stay below them and you'll stay hidden."

Kylie, Zuma, and Snouts nodded. They each carried a piece of kelp tied in a lasso loop. The other ends of the kelp were tied securely to a heavy rock formation below them.

The group split up and snuck below the stargazers. Then they slipped the lassos over the stargazers' tails, carefully avoiding the electrical barbs.

As they worked, Merliah watched the rays of

the midday sun break through the water.

As the first sunbeam inched dazzlingly toward the Emerald of the East, she heard Eris call out in triumph.

"It's time!" Eris took her seat on the throne.

"It's time!" Merliah repeated to Kylie.

The girls snuck up behind two stargazers, lassos in hand. In one quick motion, they slipped their lassos around the stargazers' necks. They pulled tight on their ropes and swung onto the backs of the fish.

The stargazers reared up like untrained stallions. They bucked and dove, trying to fling the girls off.

But Kylie and Merliah kept their kelp reins under control. The chaos caused Eris to look away from the sun.

"What's going on? Merliah?" she thundered when she saw her niece.

Eris threw several bolts of magic in the princess's direction, but Merliah dodged them, riding her stargazer like a surfboard.

The ambassadors cheered from their cage. Their princess was here to rescue them!

Chapter 21

While Merliah headed toward Eris, Kylie struggled to stay in control of her stargazer.

"Work the reins, Kylie!" Merliah called, just as her own stargazer smashed into a rock in an attempt to send her flying.

Merliah focused her attention on the beast beneath her.

"You need to listen to *me*," she said firmly. With a mighty tug, she brought her stargazer under control and zoomed toward Eris.

The midday sun inched closer to the first Mercropolis gem.

"Just a few minutes now," Eris murmured from her seat on the throne.

She blasted a few dark magic bolts toward Merliah, but her aim was off.

Alistair swam over to the other stargazers. "What are you overgrown anchovies waiting for, a written invitation? The great Eris commands you: get Merliah and her friend!"

The stargazers lunged toward Merliah and Kylie, taking their prongs off the cage bars. But they had forgotten the lassos tied to their tails. They reached the end of their kelp leashes and were jerked back.

Zuma and Snouts high-fived each other.

Mirabella was the first to realize that the cage had lost its electric force field.

"The cage!" she shouted. "Everyone work together! Push!"

The ambassadors and their aides pushed on the cage with all their might. It rose ever so slighty off the ground.

"Almost!" Selena cried.

Zuma and Snouts raced over to help.

Together with the ambassadors, they put everything they had into lifting the heavy metal cage. Soon the cage toppled over and the ambassadors raced out.

"Thank you, Zuma," Selena said.

Zuma stared at the ambassador.

"Selena?" she asked. She recognized Selena's voice, but the ambassador didn't look the same.

Selena touched her face self-consciously. "Long story," she replied. Then she waved to the other ambassadors. "Come! We must stop Eris."

As the ambassadors prepared for action, one of the stargazers broke loose and headed right toward them!

Selena barked out new orders. "Change of plans. We split up. Everyone else keep the stargazers occupied."

She took off toward the throne with Zuma and Mirabella racing behind her.

Meanwhile, Merliah and Kylie were locked in a fierce battle with Eris.

"Don't do this, Eris!" Merliah cried.

"And who's going to stop me?" Eris replied.

Merliah charged toward Eris just as the evil mermaid shot a giant bolt of magic at her. Merliah sliced through the water to avoid being knocked off balance.

The glint from the moving sun, inching closer to the first gem, caught Eris's eye for a moment.

Kylie saw her chance. She steered her stargazer just close enough.

Bzzzt!

She gave Eris an electric jolt strong enough to daze her. Eris slid from the throne and drifted down to the ocean floor.

"Yes!" shouted Merliah.

She leaped off her fish, and it turned on her to attack. Selena slipped onto its back and quickly steered the stargazer away.

"Thank you," said Merliah.

"At your service, Your Highness," Selena called over her shoulder.

Merliah took her place on the empty throne.

But Eris had not come all this way to give up. "No!" she cried. She shot a bolt of magic, aimed perfectly at Merliah.

Kylie reacted with lightning-quick speed. She steered her stargazer straight into the path of Eris's magic.

"Kylie!" Merliah screamed.

The bolt struck the stargazer with full force. A cloud of magic swirled around it. When the cloud cleared, the stargazer was gone. In its place was the fish's own worst nightmare: a beautiful, shiny seashell. It floated harmlessly to the ocean floor.

In the sudden flurry of magic, Kylie bumped her head on a piece of coral and was knocked out. She drifted into a bed of kelp.

Chapter 22

Eris again set her sights on Merliah.

"Get off that throne!" she growled, hurling more magic in the princess's direction.

Just then, the ruler of the stargazers arrived. He was still a tiny green fish.

"You!" he shouted when he spotted Eris, his voice still deep. He swam into the path of Eris's next magic ray and blasted into an even smaller version of himself. "Oh, man, not again!" he cried.

Selena, Zuma, and Mirabella leaped between Eris and Merliah. They used rocks and coral to block Eris's magic as fast as she could hurl it.

Merliah watched as the sunbeam hit the first gem. While the ambassadors deflected Eris's magic, Snouts and the aides fought off the stargazers with kelp whips and pieces of coral. They just had to hang on long enough for the sunbeam to reach the throne with Merliah seated on it.

"Give it up, Eris! It's over!" Merliah shouted as the sun bounced off the first gem and moved on to the second.

"Never!" Eris called. She aimed a bolt of magic at the third gem, blasting it to smithereens as the sunbeam inched closer to it.

Selena, Mirabella, and Zuma gasped.

"What have you done?" Merliah cried. "You'll destroy the ocean!"

"Get off the throne and maybe I can fix it," Eris said darkly.

Merliah froze, uncertain what to do.

Suddenly, Kylie darted up from the ocean floor with the shiny seashell that had been her stargazer. She placed it in the third gem's spot just in time.

The sunlight bounced off the seashell and onto the fourth gem. Then it began to move toward the throne.

Eris whipped around, confused.

The ambassadors saw their chance and lunged toward Eris, pinning her arms behind her. Unable to fire her magic, Eris struggled in vain as the sunlight hit the throne.

Merliah braced herself as she repeated the oath.

"With the changing of the tides,
Merillia power will arise.
The royal mermaid on the throne,
her fullest merself now is known!"

But nothing happened.

"Why isn't it working?" she asked.

Eris cackled bitterly.

"You have no tail!" she shouted. "You can't activate the throne! Now get out and let me sit or *no one* gets Merillia!"

"Don't do it!" Kylie called.

She rushed toward the princess, took the necklace off her own neck, and quickly put it on Merliah's.

Merliah looked gratefully at Kylie.

"I wish to become a mermaid!" she cried.

Instantly, Merliah's tail returned. She repeated the oath, and the throne was suddenly bathed in a glowing bubble of lights and colors. Waves of Merillia surrounded her.

Mirabella, Selena, and Zuma gazed at the scene before them, loosening their hold on Eris.

Eris didn't waste time. She zipped out of the ambassadors' grasp and headed straight for Merliah.

"Nooooo!" Eris yelled.

She shot a magic blast toward the princess, but it was no match for the swirl of Merillia surrounding Merliah.

The magic blast bounced off the Merillia like a rubber ball—right back at Eris! It hit the evil mermaid full force, sending her into a bed of kelp, unconscious.

Suddenly, all of her worst-nightmare spells came undone. Selena once again became beautiful, Renata regained her bravery, Mirabella's force field disappeared, and Kattrin found her speed. Even the lead stargazer returned to his normal form and size.

On the throne, the lights and colors faded.

Merliah looked down in amazement.

Her hair and tail had grown longer and more glorious, and her mermaid markings were even more brilliant than ever.

But then she remembered Kylie.

Without the necklace, Kylie could no longer breathe underwater.

Chapter 23

"Kylie!" cried Merliah. She raced to her friend and slipped the necklace around her neck.

With her last bit of energy, Kylie mumbled, "I wish to become a mermaid."

The magic kicked in and Kylie transformed back into a mermaid. Gasping for breath, she looked at Merliah.

"How did we do?" she asked.

Merliah grinned. "It was a perfect ten."

Just then, Merliah heard a familiar voice behind her.

"It was better than that. You saved us all."

"Mom!" Merliah cried. She turned to see Calissa, freed from Eris's nightmare spell, swimming toward her. The ambassadors, Zuma, and Snouts were right behind her.

Merliah raced toward her mother and almost knocked her down with a huge hug.

"I'm so proud of you," Calissa said. She reached out and pulled Kylie into their hug, too. "Both of you."

Seeing his chance to join the winning team, Alistair swam toward Calissa. "I am, too, actually!" he cooed. "Was on your side all the time, really. A double agent, you could call me. Working the angles, waiting for the moment I could help the cause the most."

Calissa gave Alistair a sideways glance. "Selena!" she called.

On cue, Selena grabbed Alistair and held him captive. She looked closely at the rainbow fish. "You are beautiful," she said with a sly smile. "If you're lucky, I'll make you a pet."

"I—I can do pet," Alistair stammered nervously.

Kattrin looked toward the stargazers. "What do we do with them?" she asked.

The lead stargazer, no longer the tiny fish of his nightmares, spoke. "I'll handle them. They'll cause you no more trouble."

"Thank you," Calissa replied. She nodded

toward the aides, who untied the stargazers.

"And if it's all right with you," the lead stargazer continued, "I'd like to handle her as well." He loomed over Eris.

As she regained consciousness, Eris looked up and yelped. She tried to blast the stargazer with her now-useless magic, but nothing happened. "Wait . . . I don't understand. . . . My magic!" she said, panicked.

The lead stargazer grinned.

"Please, leave her to us," Calissa requested. "I have a feeling she's already paying for what she did."

Reluctantly, the lead stargazer nodded. "As you wish," he said.

Eris glared at Calissa. "Don't do me any favors, sister," she sneered. "I'm not done with you yet." She rose from the kelp bed. Everyone around her gasped.

"Eris!" Merliah cried. "You have *legs*!"

"How fitting," Calissa commented. "You're now trapped in your *own* worst nightmare."

Eris's eyes grew wide with terror. "My spell . . . but then I'm like this . . . *forever*?" Eris fell to her knees and cried, "Noooo!"

Calissa looked from Eris to the ambassadors. "I trust you'll take care of her?"

"It will be our pleasure," Selena replied. "We'll find a place for her that's even more secure than a whirlpool."

Calissa nodded, satisfied. Then she turned to Merliah, who was still a mermaid. "So . . . how do you feel?" she asked.

"All right, I think," replied Merliah.

"You look amazing," Kylie said to the princess.

"Thanks," said Merliah, looking down at her tail. "I guess I won't be surfing anymore."

"I'm so sorry, Merliah. I never wanted this to happen," Calissa said softly.

"I know," Merliah replied. Then she grinned at Kylie. "Which means you'll be the one winning the Invitational!"

Kylie gave a half smile. "Merliah, come on. . . . I don't even want to think about the Invitational. It wouldn't be right."

"Are you kidding?" Merliah cried. "It's *exactly* right. I chose to give up my legs. But that means it's even more important for you to go out there and surf. You're doing it for the both of us."

Kylie's eyes twinkled. "You're sure?" she asked. "Do we even have enough time to get there?"

Calissa clapped her hands in excitement. "With all three of our tails working together? Count on it."

Kylie grinned. "Let's go."

"We'll come, too," Zuma called. "Wouldn't miss it for the world. Right, Snouts?"

The sea lion barked and rolled over happily, and the friends took off through the ocean.

Chapter 24

When they neared the shore, Merliah and Kylie popped to the surface of the water and looked around. Calissa, Snouts, and Zuma emerged behind them. They could see the crowd gathered for the Invitational on the shore. They listened as the announcer came over the loudspeaker.

"Time for the final heat in this Invitational, where we *should* be seeing Kylie Morgan and Merliah Summers . . . but the VIPs are MIA! Unless they show up ASAP, they'll get the big DNF!"

Kylie and Merliah exchanged a look.

"Guess I'd better go," Kylie said.

If she didn't show up for the final heat, she would be disqualified, earning a DNF, or Did Not Finish.

"I wish to be a human," she said.

As Kylie took off the necklace, her tail turned back into legs. She began to tread water.

"Here," Kylie handed the necklace to Calissa, but the queen put a hand on Kylie's arm.

"No. The necklace is yours now," said Calissa.

"Mine?" Kylie asked.

Calissa nodded. "You've proven where your heart truly lies."

Merliah agreed. "We never could have saved the ocean without you, Kylie."

"And we need another ambassador," Calissa continued. "Someone who experiences the ocean from above the water, not only below it. Will you help us?"

Kylie was stunned. It seemed too good to be true. But one look at Merliah's and Calissa's faces and she knew they were serious.

"I would be honored . . . Your Highnesses," she replied with a bow.

"Surfers, hit the waves!" the announcer's voice boomed through the air.

Kylie took a deep breath.

"Better run," she said. Then Kylie turned and

swam quickly toward the shore.

Calissa looked sadly at Merliah. "Are you okay?" she asked her daughter.

Merliah nodded. "Totally. It's a shame, though. I had a sweet new trick planned for today's run. I wish I could still change back so I could show it to Kylie."

As she said the words, Merliah looked down in shock. Her tail had transformed into legs!

"Mom! Kylie!" she cried in surprise.

Kylie spun around.

"Your tail!" she gasped.

"My legs!" Merliah shouted.

"I thought they were gone forever!" Kylie called.

"Me too!" Merliah replied. "I don't understand."

Calissa smiled.

"It must be the ritual," she said. "It *did* transform you into your fullest self, but your fullest self is naturally *both* a mermaid and a human."

Merliah opened her eyes wide.

"You mean . . . I can be both?"

"Apparently so," Calissa replied. "You've always been both. But now you don't need a necklace to help you change."

Merliah realized what this meant.

"I can surf!" she cried excitedly.

"You can surf in the meet!" Kylie exclaimed. "Come on!"

Chapter 25

On the beach, Fallon and Hadley watched the surfers rock the waves. Fallon's cell phone rang. It was Break, calling on his videophone to watch the meet.

"She said she'd be back for the finals," Fallon said. It wasn't like Merliah not to show up—especially because this competition was so important to her.

"No sweat, surfette," Break replied. "If she's not there, it's because Calissa needs her."

"I guess," Fallon said, sighing. "I just hope she's all right."

"She is," said Hadley. "I'm sure of it."

Suddenly, the announcer called out. "I can't believe it!" he exclaimed. "Merliah Summers and Kylie Morgan have just appeared on the waves!"

Fallon scanned the ocean's surface. "They have?" she asked.

Hadley pointed madly at the water. "Yes!" she cried.

"Groovy," said Break. "I knew she'd make it."

"Don't look now," continued the announcer, "but they're about to face the largest beast of a wave I've ever seen!"

Out on the water, Kylie and Merliah looked back and spotted a huge wave.

"Whoever tames this one will take the meet," said Kylie.

"You want it?" Merliah asked.

"Oh, yeah. You?" Kylie replied.

"You better believe it," Merliah said as she began to paddle. "May the best surfer win!"

The girls turned their boards and paddled out to meet the giant wave.

On the shore, the announcer could hardly contain his excitement. "This is one bonzer of a wave, and Summers and Morgan *both* want to wrestle it into submission!"

The crowd watched as Kylie and Merliah prepared to tackle the same wave.

The announcer gave the crowd a play-by-play. "Merliah executes a perfect aerial barrel roll, while Kylie nails a perfect floating roundhouse cutback! But wait, what's happening with Merliah Summers?"

At the sound of Merliah's name, Kylie looked behind her. Glittering magic danced all around Merliah.

"Merliah?" she called.

"It's beautiful!" Merliah called back. "I'm making Merillia!"

"But the finals?" Kylie shouted.

"This is better than the contest!" replied Merliah.

Kylie smiled at her friend. "Then I'm going to take it home!" she called.

"Go for it!" Merliah exclaimed as she cut into and out of the wave with magic shimmering all around her. She heard the announcer's voice trying to explain what was happening.

"It's almost like Merliah Summers is ... *playing*

in the waves . . . like ballet on water! I've never seen anything like it.

"But Kylie Morgan is grabbing this heat and holding it tight! She is unstoppable! Ladies and gentlemen, we might have a new Queen of the Waves!"

Fallon flinched at the announcer's words. "Ouch. Liah's got to hate that."

Break chuckled into the videophone. "Look at her, man. Does it look like she hates it?"

Just then, an air horn blew.

"That's the heat!" the announcer called. "Surfers, come on in!"

Kylie and Merliah rode to shore together. As they walked onto the beach, the crowd went wild. They surrounded Kylie, peppering her with questions and congratulations.

"Kylie! Look over here, please!" cried a photographer.

"Amazing run, Kylie!" a reporter said. "Can you tell us about your technique? How did you prepare for this incredible heat?"

Merliah looked at Kylie and beamed. Then she walked through the crowd to find Fallon and

Hadley. She threw her arms around her friends.

Break's voice came through Fallon's phone. "Everything go okay, little grommet?"

Merliah laughed at the sound of her grandpa's voice and hugged Fallon's phone for good measure.

"Better than okay!" she cried.

Then they heard the announcer again.

"The judges needed exactly zero seconds to call that one. In first place of the World Championship Surf Invitational is . . . Kylie Morgan!"

Merliah jumped up and down.

"Come get your trophy, Kylie!" the announcer said.

Kylie crossed the beach to Merliah. She grabbed her friend's hand and dragged her to the podium.

"What are you doing?" Merliah cried. "This is *your* moment!"

Kylie shook her head. "I already had my moment, when I helped you save the ocean. It's funny . . . I always thought that winning the Invitational would be a dream come true. And it's wonderful, but . . ." Kylie hesitated.

"I know," Merliah said. "It's not the same as what we did down there."

Kylie nodded, momentarily at a loss for words. "It's really special being a part of something bigger, you know? Thank you for helping me see that."

Merliah put her arm around Kylie. "Thank you," she replied.

Together, they climbed to the winner's podium. The announcer handed Kylie a huge shiny trophy, and the crowd went wild.

Kylie pushed the trophy toward Merliah, and they both hoisted it high above their heads, basking in the glow of their success—and their new friendship.

Surfing Glossary

180: a half spin of a surfer's board

360: a full spin of a surfer's board

aerial: a trick that involves the surfer rising into the air above the wave while standing on her board

backside air reverse: a trick that involves catching air and doing a backward 360

barrel: the hollow inside the part of a wave that's breaking; also called the tube

board: a surfboard; usually made of fiberglass

bonzer: Australian surf term meaning "remarkable" or "wonderful"

carve: to turn on a wave

catch a wave: to start riding a wave

crest: the top part of a wave

cutback: a move that switches the direction in which a surfer is surfing

drop in: to catch a wave that another surfer is already riding (considered bad surfing etiquette)

grommet: a young surfer

leash: the cord that attaches a surfboard to a surfer's leg

paddle: to lie down on a board and use your arms to move out into the ocean

stoked: really happy, excited

swell: a wave that's good for surfing

trick: a fancy surfing maneuver

trough: the bottom part of a wave

tube: the hollow inside part of a wave that's breaking; also called the barrel

wipe out: to fall off a board